P

Park Stories: Direct Hit
© Adam Thorpe 2009

ISBN: 978-0-9558761-3-4

Series Editor: Rowan Routh

Published by The Royal Parks
www.royalparks.org.uk

Production by Strange Attractor Press
BM SAP, London, WC1N 3XX, UK
www.strangeattractor.co.uk

Cover design: Ali Hutchinson

Park Stories devised by Rowan Routh

Adam Thorpe has asserted his moral right to be identified as the author of this work in accordance with the Copyright, Designs and Patents Act, 1988.

All rights reserved. No part of this publication may be reproduced in any form or by any means without the written permission of the publishers. A CIP catalogue record for this book is available from the British Library.

The Royal Parks gratefully acknowledges the financial support of Arts Council England.

Printed by Kennet Print, Devizes, UK on 100% post-consumer recycled Cyclus offset paper using vegetable-based inks.

Direct Hit

Adam Thorpe

THE
ROYAL
PARKS

Direct Hit

Miss Simkin's favourite bench, to which she had repaired every clement weekday lunchtime for fifteen years, had old-fashioned spiral arms and weathered slats, and was shadowed by a glorious elm. Set far enough back from the Serpentine's lower end not to be disturbed by squealing bathers or the customary high jinks that overtake people in rowing boats, the bench commanded a view, not only of the lake, but of the entire south-eastern corner of the park. She felt almost countrified, sitting there – as she had never felt in Sheffield, where she had been brought up by her widowed mother in somewhat straitened circumstances.

The bench was seldom occupied, even in the Season. The more obvious attractions of the proper lakeside seating-places made these appear inferior to her – even vulgar. Apart from nurses minding their tiny, sprucely-dressed charges, and the bowler-hatted office workers throwing crumbs to the waterfowl, they were mostly used by foreign tourists, romantic couples or awkwardly provincial visitors to the capital, as well as by the usual smattering of the dotty or the destitute. Miss Simkin distantly observed them all, closing her lips over her prominent teeth in what she occasionally realised, looking in her pocket mirror to powder her nose, was a grimace of disdain.

Shadowed under the great boughs of the elm, as in some ancient arched hall, her nook had something of the literary bower about it, and she would sometimes take along, instead of her usual crime novel, an anthology of poetry. Stiffened by her days spent typing to the major's ponderous dictation or poring over his archives, she would follow her lunch with a brisk walk along straight paths so familiar to her that at times the years would fall away and she would feel as fresh and provincial as any of the swarms of young girls with their easy manners, showily smoking in their fox-fur boas.

Then the war had come, presaged by great trenches dug across the lawns: mass graves, it was rumoured, for the coming raids' casualties. They turned out to be shelters, stinking and waterlogged. Her bench shook to the pounding of the anti-aircraft guns north of the bandstand. Soon, great hills of rubble from the cleared streets interrupted any possible view, with clouds of dissolved masonry curling from their slopes. She had watched a fleet of throbbing bombers through the bare branches of the elm, and found it remarkable that she was not afraid. Now it was all over. Three years after Victory, the dahlias were again in flower, the piggery closed, berets changed back to bowlers, and all the awfulness she had witnessed with her very own eyes seemed hardly true.

But those six serious years had swallowed up her youth. She was almost forty. When her cousin, poor dear Frederick, whom she visited every fortnight in the Star and Garter Home for totally disabled soldiers, had asked her last week whether she would ever marry, she had said (somewhat insensitively, she realised afterwards): 'Only when I find the man to fit the socks, my dear.'

And Frederick had not understood, of course. For no one ever would.

The major, even when capable of it, had never once accompanied her on her regular lunchtime excursion, though it was a matter of minutes from Lowndes Street. He referred to it as her 'private sally', and made all kinds of silly insinuations, just as he did on the rare occasions

when she took herself off for an evening out with her friend
Marjorie, or boarded the trolley-bus for Hampton Court,
or indulged in the annual motor-coach excursion into the
real countryside with the ornithology club. He even made
inappropriate suggestions when she took the electric train to
Richmond to visit Frederick.

'Frederick lost his limbs fighting for his country,'
she would say, glaring at her employer – who had received
no more hurt throughout his glorious military career than a
Mahdi spear in his rump.

She did like being alone, she insisted to herself, and
when Marjorie told her of her life with Donald and the three
children, she regretted nothing, most of the time.

It was already over a year ago, on a breezy June day
of fitful sun, that she had seen him first, as she was walking
up the path from the Albert Gate.

A gentleman – or at least a male of the species
– was sitting on the very end of her bench, apparently
slumbering over tightly-folded arms. He was dressed in a
slate-grey macintosh, with a black felt hat – the type they
called the 'Anthony Eden' – tipped over his face. She went
off and found a chair near the empty bandstand, feeling
disgruntled and uneasy as she ate her sandwich, like a
homing pigeon denied its perch. A keeper came up and
charged her tuppence.

The invader was still there half an hour later, only
wide awake: catching her eye as she walked past, he raised
his hat, and this struck her as provocative. She left the park
as usual by the Mount Street gate and arrived home ten
minutes early: a fact remarked on by the major from his
Bath chair. An elderly workman with a droopy moustache
had been spraying tar over the gravel by the dolphin
fountain, and her blouse had picked up the acrid stench.
The major remarked on that, too. 'Like cordite,' he growled.
'Bombing again, are they?' 'This is 1949, major.' 'No sense of

humour, girl!' he bellowed, as had long been his wont.

Struggling to sleep that night, the heart of the diminishing Empire beating heedlessly beyond the shutters of her room, she suddenly thought, as in an old poem: *My nook hath become a stranger's lair.*

The next day was very fine, and she had the bench to herself. She was relieved. The man was no doubt a passing bird: probably a foreigner, with exaggerated rules of politeness. She found a crumpled receipt from Boots and a 4d tube ticket left on the slats. They were not necessarily his, for the park keepers were assiduous about litter, but it was an odd coincidence. There were, generally, no signs of occupation.

Her great fear was that the bench, being old and so little used, would at some point be taken away. She looked up from her book into the giddying, ever-arching boughs of the elm, replete with fresh leaves, and closed her eyes. She decided that, if this horror were to happen, she would write a letter to the Park authorities. This was England, after all, and despite the modern determination not to preserve the rural amenities, along with the dubious new powers of Ministries and their austere Orders and Regulations, the utility of this bench would be thoroughly affirmed.

Of a sudden she felt it move and, startled, opened her eyes.

The Anthony Eden hat was on his lap, and his hair was oiled and neat, like a clerk's – its blackness no doubt artificial. She suspected him to have common vowels (hers having long been vanquished by elocution lessons). She noted a cavernous cheek roofed by prominent bone.

She looked the other way, firmly, as one does in the capital when sharing a seat. She heard the snap of a case and, stealing a glance, saw that he had donned a pair of perfectly circular spectacles. They flashed the light as he turned suddenly towards her, deliberately catching her out! She dropped her eyes to her page as he said, in the voice of a refined Englishman: 'You also are something of a book lover, I see.'

Was there just a hint of foreignness in the exaggerated care of those syllables? At the very least, she was abashed at his ignorance of the unspoken rule that respectable persons sharing any seat, whether in a park, a tram, a motor-coach or a railway carriage, should not ordinarily engage in conversation. If this were not the case, life would be made intolerable.

Once and only once, during an early bombing raid, she and the major had sheltered with Rosie the maid in a tube railway tunnel, wherein hundreds of their fellow citizens of all classes were likewise ensconcing themselves with blankets for the night. In the novelty of the situation, people were conversing with those nearest them – if only to argue. The differentiation of superiors and inferiors had evaporated: she found herself spending the night squeezed between the maid and a Cockney coalman, whose snores exuded a fume of spirits detectable even over the packed tunnel's suffocating stench.

Something of that dreadful, sleepless night came back to her now, and she gave a tiny, involuntary shudder, pretending not to hear. Naturally, she felt uncivil.

The bench gave a little admonishing jolt as he left. Her eyes surreptitiously followed him. He did not once look back, but walked unhurriedly alongside the Serpentine, pausing only to watch two boats, oars whirring like windmills, collide softly with the usual attendant squeals. It was impossible to gauge his expression from that distance, and his angular limbs gave no clue.

Inevitably, he came into her dreams that night, and rather unpleasantly. He was there in the park, in his dark macintosh, pointing into a trench shelter, which was almost full. 'No,' she tried to shout, her voice too hoarse to be heard, anticipating the direct hit as if it was still to happen, as if she had not yet picked herself up from the gutter in Mount Street (wherein she had dived) and walked towards the aftermath in a daze: the cries and moans, clothes blown clean off, hands and legs caught high in the branches, the dying carried away on sheets of corrugated iron, the man with half a face asking her for a cigarette. Her own face was already smarting, and when she looked in her pocket mirror, she saw it was starred with embedded glass. She woke up in a frightful state, the wailing of a siren dying away in her ear. This was silly. The most she had ever suffered was conjunctivitis from either the dust or smoke and nausea from the broken gas-pipes.

So she ate her sandwich on the Monday following with a nervousness she had never felt during the war itself. The weekend rain had cleared to fine weather, and the park's foliage was draped in glittering tiaras of wet: a wood-wren shook its tiny wings free of diamonds not two feet away. She had brought along a murder mystery she presently started, sitting on her macintosh against the wet; she wondered what the mysterious gentleman would do if he came up now, for the macintosh occupied the full length of the bench.

Wearing her stouter boots for the puddled paths, she walked more briskly than usual, pausing only to watch an American couple launch themselves into the Serpentine with excessive fuss, gawped at by a troop of barefoot school truants with a sugar-box cart. Such is a park's undiscerning democracy, she thought – like the top of a motor-bus, like the falling of bombs.

The bowling green was in use, the bowls sending

up a thin tail of spray as they rolled, the two couples laughing coarsely for their hour's sixpence. She remembered the sheep gathering upon it in more serious times, prior to being shorn, their fleeces destined for the flying jackets of brave young airmen. How she had dreamed of meeting a brave young airman! But that was what Marjorie had done, for Donald was in Lancasters, and now he was a drunk with twitches and a shiny, burned face. Far better to remain independent, to be the habitué of one's own interior haunts. How lucky she was, really, not to be enduring the thankless drudgery of the average modern housewife, battling with utilitarian meals under the watchful eye of the Ministry of Food.

'How really very lucky I am,' she reflected, watching the jets of water shatter endlessly upon the dolphin atop her favourite fountain, its romance separated from the public by a broad circle of forbidden turf: the surrounding tar had set, yet was still sticky underfoot. She pictured last week's workman in his leather apron, the pipe coiling from the huge wheeled tank with its sombre and vicious stink – and thought it less real than the major's account of Omdurman. She noticed someone walking on the very perimeter of the grass, just within the ankle-high rail.

It was him. He was walking towards her with a book in his hand, nearing her on the circle like some awful figure on a clock.

'I believe this is yours,' he said, stepping carefully over the metal rail and raising his hat. He had no socks. She saw this as she looked down, taking the book in a fluster of apologies. It was the crime novel, unfortunately: *The Poisoned Chocolates Case* by Anthony Berkeley. She thanked him and drew herself up and glanced towards the comforting proximity of Park Lane, where the incessant traffic rolled. Fancy having no socks. No doubt his ankles were as skeletal as his wrists.

'The title was most tempting,' he continued. 'But valour overcame curiosity.'

She avoided his eye, her heart thudding furiously. Valour, my foot! The fervent hiss of the fountain made his words harder to hear, but there was no doubting their import. 'Do you think,' he said, glancing at his shoes, 'we might be stuck here like two elegant lampposts, if we do not move forthwith?'

She was astonished to find his hand upon her elbow, already guiding her to where the tarmacadam ended. 'I know little about crime fiction,' he was saying, 'beyond the inimitable Sherlock Holmes. Does the title in this case not somewhat prejudice the mystery?'

'I usually read poetry,' she pronounced, feeling the pressure of his fingers above the mother-of-pearl buttons on her sleeve, of which one was missing.

'Ah,' he said, releasing her arm; 'so that is why you come here every day: to read verse. You are keeping up the ebbing romance of the park.' He looked towards the broad sand-track of Rotten Row, where moist clots of horse-dung gleamed. 'My grandmother used to ride up and down in a victoria, you know, with a red-faced old coachman called Henry flicking his whip.'

He smelt faintly of lanoline soap. His glasses flashed upon her over a gallant smile. She remembered that he had no socks. One could meet anyone in a park. Over the years there had been assaults and murders among the shrubbery, it was a place of easy concealment, of nefarious and even obscene doings. Last night's dream returned, overlapping the present moment with horrible, ridiculous images that had once been as real to her as the flower-bed beyond him. It was a dream of premonitory doom.

'I am late,' she said, in a sudden breathless fluster of dread. 'You must excuse me. I am expected by my husband.'

'Your husband?'

The bare-faced untruth had the intended effect: a spasm of disappointment passed across the bony features. 'Just as well, then, I did not address you as Miss Simkin.'

She was aghast, until his thin finger prodded open the green cover of the Penguin lying in her hand, baring the first page to view. *Miss Agnes Simkin. 22 Lowndes Street, London. May 1949.* 'Permit me to congratulate you: you must be very freshly wed. I was on my way to Lowndes Street, of course. Or have you moved, now you are married?'

'Oh no,' she said, reddening.

He was looking down at the grass with a melancholic air. Of course: a widower! She felt foolish. His features just needed filling out. They were regular, even handsome. She guessed his age as late forties. Not old, for a man. His fingers had all but gripped her arm, with a man's forgetful strength. He had a very pleasant, low voice that was now saying, 'I, too, must return home.'

Oddly, she did not want him to leave. She asked if he had far to go.

He paused for a moment, his dark eyes glittering. 'Berkeley Square,' he said.

She all but gasped, having pictured a rented room in gloomy Bloomsbury, a jumble of books. 'I do hope,' she remarked hurriedly, covering her surprise, 'you are not near the so-called haunted house, at Number 50.'

'Not so very near,' he said. After a pause, as if reflecting on the propriety of it, he added: 'Number 14.'

'Oh, number 14. Not number 13, at least!'

'No indeed. I am afraid I must bid you good-day. My daughters will soon be returning from school, expecting tea. My wife despairs over the efforts of our new cook to bake even the simplest cake, given the meagre allowances at her disposal. My dog, Ruffles, is buried in the dog cemetery here. He was hit by shrapnel from a V2: you know pets weren't allowed in the shelters. My wife could not bear the name, but it is still inscribed on the tombstone. You have the loveliest eyes I have ever seen, Miss Simkin.'

He disappeared through the gate as she looked after him in open-mouthed astonishment. The last glimpse of him was a bare ankle flashing white below the bottom of his trousers: it reminded her of a magpie vanishing into woods.

On the way back to the major's, she descended from her golden cloud, and all but burst into tears. She fluffed her typing, snapped at Rosie, and was truculent over dinner as the major snorted about rationing. That night in bed she brooded. The following day, instead of entering the park, she walked up Knightsbridge and Piccadilly, bought a pair of gentleman's socks in Savile Row, and found herself – scarcely by her own volition – in Berkeley Square.

In her very first week as the major's secretary fifteen years before, not yet embarked on the voluminous and ever-ballooning memoirs, she had been taken by him on an historical tour of Mayfair, culminating in what was once the most aristocratic and elegant spot in London. 'This was once the town abode of Horace Walpole... here is number 38, from where Lord Rosebery's lovely daughter eloped... and this is 50 Berkeley Square, of haunted-house fame. All balderdash. Its ghost derives entirely from a novel by a close friend of my father's, Rhoda Broughton, and has nothing whatsoever to do with historical fact, Miss Simkin...'

She cautiously circled the great plane trees, as though being spied upon from the square's myriad tall windows. She was shocked to find Walpole's grand residence no more than a bomb-site overgrown with fireweed, and number 38 a similar void, scattered with paper litter. Number 13 (lucky after all) had a couple of small, smartly-dressed girls sitting on its chipped steps, playing with a kitten.

What ought to have been number 14 had steps, but no house. Huge wooden props supported the scarred walls of its adjoining flanks, their smart wallpaper and fine stone fireplaces open to the air. Some scruffy boys were dropping marbles into a complicated run made of metal pipes and rusty hub-caps.

Composing herself with difficulty, she asked the girls what had become of the house next door.

'Destroyed by the Germans,' they said, matter-of-factly and in unison.

'And the people living there? The family?'

'Oh, it was only sort of offices,' said the older one. 'There was nobody inside. Hit by an oil-bomb,' she added, with relish.

Miss Simkin was puzzled only for as long as it took to pick up her crime novel again. It was a week later. The grey light of London was leavened by the park's greenery. She remembered how, upon her asking him where he lived, his eyes had rested for a moment on the book by Anthony Berkeley.

She had, over the last year, attended the noisy demonstrations she would never bother with before (scanning every face), and endured the open-air orators of Speaker's Corner, who tended not to wear socks. Searching the memorials in the park's dog cemetery over and over, she had found no Ruffles.

On the bench, examining herself in her pocket mirror while powdering her nose, she wondered now if what he had said about her eyes had as little in it as anything else he had claimed.

As she returned the pocket mirror to her handbag, surreptitiously prodding the socks folded neatly within, she realised she did not really care one way or another, because to him it was the truth.